THEY DON'T MAKE PLUS SIZE SPACESUITS

ALI THOMPSON

For Josh, who makes everything possible.

TRIGGER WARNINGS AND CONTENT NOTES.

A general warning in all pieces for fatphobia and fatphobic discrimination, a discussion of weight and weight loss, descriptions of dieting.

Nothing left to burn—child abuse, abuse by a parent, verbal abuse, eating disordered behaviors, suicidal ideation, surgery reference, medical harm, coercion, self harm

You poured ashes into my mouth—emotional abuse within a romantic relationship

I'm not sorry—abusive job environment, surgery, medical coercion, physical abuse, body horror, public humiliation

We shall all be healed— surgery, medical coercion, medical trauma, self harm, body horror, emotional abuse, verbal abuse, physical abuse, state violence, public humiliation, burning, pain, PTSD, knives/cutting

FAT THE FUTURE

For a long time, I didn't notice how invisible I was.

I am used to being so very visible, the most noticeable thing in any room. It was hard to conceive of myself as invisible when I'm so often a target, in a world that goes out of its way to make sure I don't fit.

It's hard to notice the shape of the absence where you aren't allowed to imagine yourself to be.

But that was before fat activism. After the swooping, exhilarating changes, after inhaling blog posts and podcasts and photos of other fat people, breathing it in like the life giving oxygen it was, I did start to notice.

When I look into the media, I am a void. There is an invisible hole in the world where I should be, a soul-destroying lack of imagination that erases my existence.

Then the movie *Wall-E* came out. And I started to notice it more: the hateful judgments overwriting my life. Deleting me; stealing my face and putting it on the story of a doomed world.

I did not want a cute cartoon movie about robots that also hates me.

I fell in love with science fiction when I was a kid, and I fell hard. But as so often happens in the life of a fat girl, the things I loved did not love me back. These stories didn't want me, couldn't hold me.

I thought about it for a long, long time.

I returned again and again to the thought that has become a rock in my shoe. Where are all the fat girls? Where am I?

Where are the fat girls in space? Where are the fat girls in *Star Trek*? Where did we go?

Every so often, I would bring it back up. Where am I? What is my future meant to be?

Not in a dystopia where I am the visual stand-in for every wrong thing. Where can I imagine myself to be, in a world of peace and space and transporters?

And every time, someone would tell me— kindly, oh so kindly—that in a utopia, fatness wouldn't exist anymore. Because it would have been solved. I would be solved.

Solved. Solved out of existing.

These stories are born of my rage and frustration and terror.

What am I supposed to think about all these sweet, good hearted people who want to wish me out of existence? All these soft words and delicate euphemisms to build a velvet lined coffin to bury me alive.

How do they think the sickly sweetness of their deep "concern" feels to someone me? Do they even care?

Fat people exist, have always existed, will continue to exist. A culture that wishes us erased from existence is a choking poison that I am forced to breathe every single day.

I am afraid of these people and the brutality they call concern.

I don't 'feel' fat. I am fat. Not 'thin girl fishing for compliments' fat, not medium sized, but actual FAT fat. A girl whose bulk warps the fabric of thin normative minds through her sheer stubborn refusal to dissolve into thin air.

If we dream our futures into being, then I am doomed. I am gone. We are gone, where did we go, what have these people DONE with us?

And to us.

In their quest for the ever straighter and more narrow, they have hung their own sins and fears around my neck and cast me down into hell.

Their utopia would be my doom.

If they want to erase me, I intend to extract my pound of flesh before I go. Their precious future is a horror, a nightmare that I can never wake up from, and I intend to make them see that much at least, if I can.

I can't make them change their ways, but I can give them the fruit of this poisoned tree and dare them to take a bite. Dare them to see it my way, if just for a moment.

Will they? Can they?

I don't know.

It hurt me to write these stories, because they are born from my hurt. If it hurts you to read them, then you are with me. You are living my pain and my fears when these stories wound you.

This collection is for the people who need to hear that furious howl. This is for the ones who can recognize my agony.

It's not my fault or yours.

The people who hate us are the ones who are wrong.

NOTHING LEFT TO BURN

The height chart at my mother's house is tacked to the wall in the bathroom next to the sink, and every day she makes me stand in front of it. Bending down over me, she is too long and too big, and I wish on every star, on every blown out birthday candle, on my secret lists to Santa and my prayers to Jesus, that I will never grow so long as my mother.

As she squints at the numbers and turns her head this way and that, I try to slink down into the floor, shoes off bare feet so I don't accidentally claim any extra height.

Grim faced and sour, my mother silently scratches the figures into a tattered notebook, and I know I added a fraction of an inch.

I hunch down even harder and join her in her reducing exercises, working harder and harder, rolling the foam rollers over my calves and thighs until they burn and bruise, standing under the Length Smasher™ with it balanced on my head, as she piles weight after weight on top of it. The endless series of flexing and tension exercises guaranteed to pull the body down and make it lower and smaller and more beautiful.

THE EXERCISES ARE PAINFUL, but I have grown used to pain. Stoical and silent, I learn different flavors of it, the stabbing needles in my back and shoulders at night when I can finally unfold myself. The pain that slides into a constant roaring swish of hurt that seizes my body, when one day I can no longer uncrick my neck or unroll my spine. Hot pinching fingers of agony in every part of my body, but it is worth it.

Everyone folds downward, wears light colors. Light colors make you look shorter. Imagine your spine is an accordion and press it down. Only vertical stripes please; horizontal ones add height.

The illusion, darling, is the game. And it's important to know how to play the game. You may already be short, but you could always be shorter.

Try my supplements; this tea makes you lower. Don't eat greens, they increase height. Never ever drink milk—the calcium is practically decadent and who wants to wall-sit off those extra fractions of an inch?

DREAD IS a suffocating weight inside my chest at each measuring, the height chart I can never match, already to the 98th percentile. Swallowing down the shame, bitter and slimy, hunching down and low, and it's never down small enough. A rubber band pulled too tight, the snap back pain of it inevitable and unavoidable.

I imagine myself tiny, shrunken. I think constantly about

car accidents and shortening illnesses, anything to pull down the inches. I picture myself stepping in front of the car, begging for the injury.

YOU MAY BALK at the price of such beauty, but you don't understand. It's unhealthy to be so long; it causes depression and anxiety; it makes your bones more likely to break and gives you cancer and heart attacks.

I have vivid and recurring dreams of plunging my own hands into my legs and ripping out chucks of bone like modeling clay, reducing my length like some kind of height wizard. Oh, if only I could.

MOTHER BUYS every book that promises to shrink the torso, the legs, the back and arms. Mother is desperate to be short and small, and I am infected by her desperation.

She buys special food that is only for her and me, revolting and slightly metallic. The rest of the family gets to eat normal food, and I must drink two large glasses of water before I am allowed to sit down and eat my sawdust and mash, the smirking face of my sibling marking me as the family failure. They are still well under 5 feet.

THE FOOD IS SUPPOSED to block my growth hormones and absorb my bone cells so I don't continue to grow at such a fast rate. The powder claims to be a milkshake, but it never loses its gritty texture or sour aftertaste. The blocky clear nutrition bars that are the only thing Mother will pack in my lunch box, with a thermos filled with water.

Other children laugh to see me try to eat them, and so I

start throwing them away. Until one day, my teacher sends a note home, and I am grounded and marked with a palm print across my cheek. The next day that teacher can't quite look me in the eye.

IT's all for my own good.

IT's dangerous to be too long, too big. It's selfish; it steals and wastes resources that other, smaller, better people could use. How many too-long people will die each year, from not trying hard enough to make themselves shorter? And how much do they cost?

Too much.

How much do you cost to live? Too much, far too much, unless you can make yourself smaller hurry hurry it's almost too late.

MOTHER GIVES me pills to stop my growing and they smell strange and they make my heart flutter and I feel like a balloon at the end of a string and everything is a watercolor with water everywhere but only one drop of paint that shimmers and then bleeds away into almost nothing spread too thin and too weak to fight the never-ending drumbeat of smaller, shorter, smaller, reduce your length, never be so long and how long means ugly and I don't want to be ugly anymore.

· · ·

I AM TIRED. Tired all the time.

MOTHER TAKES me to a special doctor. He makes me run on a treadmill, and breathe into a special bag, and lie facedown while he does something with needles into my back that makes me scream and scream. It burns.

"LOSS OF INCHES GUARANTEED."

Mother schedules me for another appointment next month.

I AM NOW ALMOST as tall as she is.

I can see my failure reflected back in her eyes. More marks on the height chart. She takes it down now, in between measurings, because she can't stand to look at it.

"YOU AREN'T EVEN TRYING to be shorter," she screams at me one day, and I know then I will always be sad. Always long and ugly, and ugly means no one will ever love me. Not my mother, and not anyone.

The next day, a surgery brochure on my bed.

"TAKE 4 inches off your total length!" The brochure leads to a website and the website to a video, a man's voice soothing over before and after photos, height dramatically reduced, sad and long and ugly before, smiling and happy and small small short and small after.

. . .

THE PROCEDURE TO cut into the leg and break the bones, removing the too, too long pieces and sew it all back together, all described in hushed and sympathetic terms. Perfectly safe. Become a healthy new you.

I let it get so bad. How could I? Why didn't I work harder to stay small?

THE CRISP SHEETS of the hospital linen crinkle beneath my hands. I will finally become the short and small and delicate person I always knew I could be.

I will remake myself into someone who can be loved. I will be like them.

I WILL BE SMALL.

I'M NOT SORRY

I t's 8AM, and I'm already late for work when I realize I
can't get into the coffee shop. Or rather, I could go in,
but the TrackFit implanted in my forearm will start
making a godawful racket.

I'M JUST on my way back from the fasting blood glucose test,
required at my BMI every six weeks, and all I want in life is
coffee. In my rush to get out the door, I hadn't managed to
remember to bring either my thermos or my toast and jam,
both lovingly prepared by my partner, abandoned on the
kitchen counter in my morning frenzy to leave. A frenzy
made even more overwhelming today by my desperation
not to miss my city-ordered blood test or agitate my fragile
job environment any further.

"I'LL STAY LATE," I had promised my boss, his eyes slits of
suspicion and distaste. "Please, the blood test has to be first
thing, and they're usually running behind..."

"We make a lot of allowances for you." His gravel voice is like two boulders grinding together, the skin pulled taut and wrinkle free over his skull, everything smooth and blank except the rage smoldering in his eyes.

The data center is staffed with undesirables; the people who don't qualify for citizenship benefits, the ones who are accused of being a blight on paradise. The data center is boring. It pays almost nothing, especially when you compare it to a citizen's guaranteed job. We have to ask permission to use the bathroom. I am afraid that these blood tests will cost me this horrible job, and I'm not eligible for unemployment. If I refuse or forget a blood test, I could lose my health insurance, such as it is.

"Please sir," I reach for contrition, submission, begging, anything. "They're only open during the week, starting at 7:30."

"So go then." He turns away, dismissing me.

"But I have to get from there to here," I try again. "And they're late usually..." I sigh and turn away.

EVERY DAY I am supposed to take two thousand steps, as tabulated by my TrackFit's step counter, otherwise there are consequences.

Consequences like the light that beams from my skin, from strategically placed, ultra-powerful LEDs implanted under the skin of my wrists, the top of my sternum, my earlobes and my temples.

If I set foot in this coffee shop, I will light up flashing red beams from under my skin, and every wifi device within a 10 foot radius will start blaring, "Obesity, Deviant, Wasteful, Epidemic". On repeat.

It's hard to get a restaurant to serve you anything while

all that's going on. It's not illegal for me to buy food or for them to sell it to me. But it's essentially impossible.

IT'S ALL VOLUNTARY, you know. The TrackFit was voluntary, the LEDs were voluntary.

BEFORE I WAS FINALLY ASSIGNED to the data center, the employment department had said that at my BMI they couldn't guarantee me a job. The job guarantee has loopholes because it's really only a guarantee for citizens. And people who are BMI non-conforming can't be citizens.

Jobs were for the deserving people, the thin people, the people whose existence didn't make a mockery of the shortages and the hunger of people in faraway places, the people who weren't responsible for the sea level rise. Never mind that the seas had started rising decades and decades before I was born.

A scapegoat is required. A scapegoat will be provided.

The jobs would be going to the deserving and the housing would be going to the deserving and the FOOD would certainly be going to the deserving and no one no one NO ONE is less deserving than you, fat girl, so if you know what's best for you, you'll let us puncture your skin and your muscles and your mind and you'll let us turn you into an example. If you want to live you will let us.

AND SO I VOLUNTEERED.

Because it was voluntary.

. . .

THEY SWORE the tech would be light, as light as air, the air they want to turn me into. It would make me into a drop of rain, a wisp of wind, let me become lighter than air so I can fly away into oblivion.

I can feel it shifting under my skin, slithering inside me, something dark and insidious. When it malfunctions it sends small (getting larger every night) electric shocks into my nerves, crawling pain down my body and back up again, bleeding seeping battery acid through my veins and into my mouth until I could spit it in the face of the next thin person who asks me if I've heard of dieting.

Have you heard of the fat people gone missing? The ones who didn't wouldn't couldn't lose the weight? There can't be any fat people in the city, not after the decrees and the declarations. And so there aren't. Save myself and the other lonely few, the fat bodies I glimpse at a distance. The others who turn away quickly. We can't congregate. They don't want us to become more infected by admitting there are others.

IT'S for your own good. For the greater good. For whatever reason they make up this time.

EVERY MORNING the TrackFit resets my steps to zero.

There is no way to get coffee in the morning, no banked steps to apply to the next day, no averages to put toward a small no cream no sugar Americano, mostly hot water and I can't even get that, no coffee at work, I'll just have to struggle through with water.

I could wave my right arm around in wild figure eights

while I run in a circle, but I've been photographed and cited twice by concerned citizens. Those nosy busybodies shoving my feet out from under me, the screwed up fury of their faces as they glare at me. So condescending in the hatred they dare to call concern, as they rat me out to the authorities for the crime of being alive.

I'VE REPORTED the bugs in the TrackFit to the website, read all the FAQs, done the online searches and all I can come up with is that the daily reset is "a known issue." Known and ignored, like the crawling sensation inside my chest, underneath the LED in my sternum, that creeping dread that never really goes away.

Why don't I ever see any other fat people? What is the city doing with them? I wonder in my darkest, most paranoid nights if we are being harvested. To what end, I couldn't even begin to guess.

I never tell my partner this, they are dealing with enough in loving the unlovable and all I can do to repay their kindness is to do and say nothing. I work for the meager wages I can get, while waiting to disappear, like all the rest, the people we never see any more.

I SIGH and turn away from the coffee shop as I am shoved repeatedly by the people around me. Their thin, angry faces, predators who can't look at me with anything other than a lust to see me destroyed, beaten, bloody, torn apart.

I turn away from the smell of coffee and trudge back to the entrance of the glass coffin skyscraper where I spend most of my waking hours. I'll try a street cart for lunch, they'll sell anything to anyone.

．　．　．

IS THIS PARADISE? The giant signs everywhere say yes, but I wonder.

I haven't lost a single pound. I hope I never do.

It doesn't matter anyway, it never did.

YOU POURED ASHES INTO MY MOUTH

I've been reduced down to one meal a day.

Two lunar cycles ago, I was reduced down to one meal plus. The plus being a small snack cube in the afternoon. I hate the dull brown and tacky sticky snack cubes, only as big as the smallest joint in my pinky. I hate their seaweed smell. I hate how they are slightly sweet but also slightly meaty.

If someone made a paste of dates and catfish, it might come close. Appalling that I might come to miss that taste, although I suspect I will.

It's kind of amazing how my brain can still pick out individual flavors when it's been years since I had a meal made of anything resembling food. The burnt metal and chalk taste floats underneath the vitamin shakes they deliver once a seven day. The sour waxy fake chocolate and the bitter coating the sweetener leaves in my mouth.

I try to rinse it out, but by the time it goes, it's practically time for another dose.

. . .

I GUESS I must have passed over a new scale plate hidden underneath the sidewalk. Probably somewhere in the plaza, where they were working on it a few weeks back. I thought I'd mapped out all the scales. I work hard to avoid them.

It's a foolish game. They'll have me eventually. I know that. I've known that for as long as I can remember.

When the latest meal reduction message flashes across my visual implant, my legs fold up of their own accord. I sit down flat on the floor. For a while, I just sit and stare with my back tucked against our bed. I stare at the steel grating across from me, a decorative silver panel with tiny holes in it, set back slightly from the otherwise gleaming expanse of white walls.

I have a recurring impulse to thread tiny things into the little holes, bits of wire or paper, little pieces of string, but Caro scolds me and takes them all down.

MY THOUGHTS ARE faint and slow underneath the rushing in my ears and the tight squeezing band of fear that crushes my head. I think about how badly I'd wanted the flat silver gray inset to have something restful to look at, a break from all the polish and reflective surfaces.

About how I'd had to plead with Caro. About how she'd finally given in, although I know it still offends her sense of normalcy. I wonder if she'll have it taken out once I'm finally gone.

I wish I'd been able to keep the kitten I'd found last year, but Caro made a report and it was gone by morning. I can still feel the hollow, scooped out place in my chest from where the kitten had sat, warm and purring. Maybe I'll see him again, maybe they'll take to where he is. I wonder if my kitten will remember me. If anyone will.

She's very by the book, is Caro. I think she reported me last quarter when I'd had to start insetting panels into my clothes. I'd tried to hide the patches, make the stitching small, but of course she knew.

SOMEONE TOLD.

I had to add the panels as I could barely move for fear of bursting a seam. I couldn't even breathe. It's been such a long time since I could breathe.

I was called to a resident manager meeting to be dress-coded. Out of regulation. They tsked and clucked and finally found me the shapeless baggy gray outfit I am now required to wear.

It stands out in a sea of never ending white cloth— flowing ivory, woven cream, pin-tucked bone.

Once I caught a glimpse of another figure in gray, far away. I had started to go after them, a sprint caught in my bunched muscles as Caro gripped my wrist.

"I love you," she'd said with her mouth, but her eyes said 'stop embarrassing me'.

She should have left me long ago, but Caro is very loyal. She reminds me she is loyal. She had prospects and will have prospects.

IT'S ALL SO VERY slow. I wish they would hurry up. I wonder if it will happen faster if I just decide not to get up from this bed. I'm sure Caro would report that too.

Because she loves me. She says she loves me.

My food rations have been cut and cut again. I am on work detail and then double work detail.

I am a bag shaped like a person, blown up full of air, thinned at the edges and starting to fade.

I am ready to go now.

I don't know where they take the aberrant, the ones who can't obey, but I am ready to go there. I'm not going to get up from this spot until they take me there.

Take me today.

There is no fatness in Eden. Those problems have been solved.

WE SHALL ALL BE HEALED, AT LAST, AT LAST

I check my phone, looking for any calls for help in my sector. They're coming up less and less recently, and since Cin keeps promising that we'll be leaving— really leaving forever any day now— I can't help but wonder if the two are related. Will the day truly come when we aren't needed any longer?

A little nervous, a little bored, the usual in our work. I rub the back of my neck, under my borrowed long hair, the wig a light purple and blue with cascading perfect corkscrew curls. My fingers trace the thick ridge of scar tissue, and I scowl down at my thick black boots.

I'd gone in for a visual implant and a wifi upgrade and came out with a "complimentary" spinal bypass, my vagus nerve connected to a health center where they could control my hunger signals, "for (my) own good." They stopped asking us if we want the surgery. Now all surgeries are The Surgery, and there's so many varieties.

THE BOX STOOD out against the skin of my neck, jutting out

hard edges where none should exist. When they said I could grow my hair out to hide it, I shaved my head instead.

In my darkest moments, a blade poised to dig out the rigid square object, no matter the cost, but they could tell, they could always tell. And the device would activate, slithering and buzzing. I would put my whole soul into screaming, but only a tiny, high pitched wheeze would come out.

The clicking never quite stopped. It was intermittent but I swear I could hear it even though they all said I was a liar.

"It doesn't do that," said the thin doctor who doesn't have an override button soldered into her spinal cord, hijacking her nervous system. I think she must have been able to feel the murder in my glare, because she fiddles with her phone and I am overtaken. The little box in the back of my neck beeps once and then invisible giant hands work my lungs like an accordion. Repulsive.

The deep breathing is supposed to make me relax. They won't stop until I'm relaxed. So I unclench my jaw, and I smile.

I smile until my head detaches itself from my body, rearing back and forth on its own to spew rage and bile and fury and destruction through this doctor's office and out into the street. I don't look at the doctor; the resentment is too strong behind my eyes.

I AM AN UNSOLVABLE PROBLEM. I am a future that shouldn't exist and yet I AM HERE.

I am always hungry, but never for the food that sits like ashes on my tongue. They said that the damage to my sense of taste was an accident, but I've never believed it. The texture of food is wrong, all grotesque and too large, no amount of chewing can resolve it.

I starve. I suffocate. And I've never lost a single pound.

Maybe one day Cin and the rest of our crew will let me kill my old doctor. I sigh, check my phone one more time. Probably not.

ON UTOPIA, happiness is guaranteed, but only to the thin ones, the BMI approved, and the rest of us can eat dust and spider webs and die. Happiness is a stick they use to beat you with, a promise they will never fulfill, not until you have made yourself a small cringing shadow of a person, carved up your own soul and sliced it into fine, even pieces.

(Now that we've taken control of your hunger, aren't you happy, Kit? Why won't you be happy and smile smile smile. Such a pretty face. What a shame. Smile.)

(Ungrateful.)

Every so often, the most half assed "article" will mention the fat people gone missing, and where pray tell are they going? Couples and siblings, parents and children, sometimes entire friend families, just zip. Gone.

It's always met with a shrug. Since transport became (mostly) easy for people (the rich and the criminal, what's the difference) they said it's too hard to track people. They could be parsecs away, who cares? The ones who want to come back, will come back.

That makes me grin. Because no one comes back from where we send them. Why would they ever want to?

I'M GETTING AHEAD of and behind myself. My name is Kit and I help us, the fat ones. Sometimes I get to actually physically fight for us and those are pleasing days. This is my third run back to Utopia, the hellhole where I was born but no longer have to live. A gilded artwork of a planet, the shining surface gleam hiding the rot, but not very well. You can always smell it underneath.

The phone buzzes in my hands, and I look at the message. We'll be off soon. No new pick ups today, either the need is getting less desperate (doubtful) or they've blocked our counter-propaganda distribution again. Or something worse, and people are too afraid.

It's shocking what people will do when they're too afraid. Well. It should be shocking but really isn't anymore.

I feel a little pang, and I can't tell if the twinge is just disappointment, or the scar tissue acting up again. I see a bright flicker in the distance. I squint a little and see Dis, hand raised to wave at me. It's a little far for me, but I always turn off my vision implant when we come to Utopia because they've hijacked me enough, thank you very much.

Dis says that it's a standard issue implant and that I might as well use it, because no one can hack an eye implant, but xie's never felt what it feels like to have someone else working your lungs from outside your body, so Dis can mind xer own damn business.

Their glances catch and snag on each other, Dis and Em, when they think I can't see. But this job is what I am good at. It's what I live for. I raise my hand to wave back and then circle back around to my transfer point.

JUST A LITTLE HOP, skip and a jump, Cin had said that first time, after they put their arms underneath my faintly twitching body and pulled me up to safety. Slumped over next to the cement stairs, underground in the subway, they had found me before I could be swept up and away, out of view.

I had a little bracelet I used to wear, it said "Vagus Nerve" on it in large letters, so people would know it was just the tech, you see, and not a real seizure or a real vagrancy.

Not that it ever mattered.

As for what really happens when you are forced in public to take deep starving breaths, the whistling heave of them past gritted teeth, dropping everything from suddenly nerveless hands while you swear, you swear in your head you can hear them all laughing, back at the health control headquarters or maybe that's just the people who have gathered, sensing prey.

Utopians are natural predators. As for what comes next... You know what can happen. No need to spell it out.

I DON'T LET myself remember that. Instead, I think of the day that the person standing over me was Cin. Even through my panic, and the pain in my arm where it hit the concrete as I went down (side effects), I was so shocked to see another fat person, and so close.

(Every surgical procedure has side effects, Kit, and you should thank us for trying to help you at all.)

In those days, I only ever saw other fat people at a distance, disappearing around a corner, eyes averted on the train, pressed backwards, curled in small, as small as small can go.

Cin wasn't like that. They leaned down next to me, and smiled sweet and easy like a crisp day in Fall. "Hey there, friend." Soft and slow, a tone for soothing a wounded animal.

I am captivated by the gentle slopes of their face in its full roundness, the delicate point of their chin making the curve below it seem ever softer and more beautiful. A wave of dark curling hair sweeps from left to right and flops in their dark eyes a little.

I don't remember what else they said to me, but I remember them helping me to my feet, hoisting my leaning weight against their solid one. I was a boneless rag doll in their arms, but the fear left me. I wanted to go with them, wherever they were going.

I still do.

A STUDY of convex and concave, Cin is a series of loops and turns, solid and gorgeous, their every arch and bend a marvel.

Cin half dragged me to the transport site and took me back with them to the Taget base. They held my hand through the implant removal, talking to me in that same mesmerizing tone.

I don't know how to be kind, never learned the way of it. I am spiky and furious and I often think maybe I shouldn't have survived everything I have. But at the end of the day, I am proud to be alive.

On the first day of my real life, I saw everything I had ever hoped for, everything that I had longed for and dreamed of and more, become my reality.

EVERYONE LOVES CIN, and why wouldn't they? I do. Just as much as anyone, but maybe a little more. Foolish, I snarl at myself, but the warm beam of their smile tugs at me, just under my ribs. I don't blame myself, try not to blame myself for this ridiculous crush.

Em doesn't think I can hear it when she calls me broken

and the other things, says that I am out of control, danger-ous. Em is a good pilot, but I still hate her for talking to Cin about me in that low, urgent voice, the smug certainty of hers that makes me want to hit things. And I worry that she will talk Cin out of smiling at me or folding me in their arms. I don't like touching or hugging but I crave it from Cin.

I tell Em to mind her own damn business. Then I smile at her with a broken glass smile, because what's she going to do, report me for smiling? I think she gets my meaning because it hasn't happened again.

THEY SAID I had to be awake when they took the implant out. I still dream about it, pain so bad it's become colors. The smell of myself burning. They are burning me, and I scream until my voice gives out. I can only make low, hurt animal noises after that. When I don't take anything before sleep-ing, I dream about it all. The scars take a long time to heal, will maybe never really be completely healed.

I always take a sedative now before sleeping.

The therapist on Taget says that three years is not such a long time, not for such an extreme case and that the edges of all of this will dull over time. I find that almost impossible to believe.

There are a lot of therapists on Taget. The need is great.

I have a standing invitation to move on to our perma-nent new home, a place prepared for me to rest, but when Cin goes on rotation, I want to go too. I want to help.

I want to see the hope come back into their eyes.

LITTLE MESSAGES, left were you can read them if you know

how, tell of a place where fat people can just live. One day, we will all be together and on that day? We will heal each other. At last.

I can take you there. We can help each other. Just reach out your hand.

ACKNOWLEDGMENTS

My first thanks has to go to my husband, Josh. Thank you for washing dishes, feeding cats, and for everything else that you do to make the space for me to pursue my creative dreams. My life with you is filled with joy and delight.

Another thank you to Josh for your constructive and precise copy editing. I couldn't have done this without you. Every day with you gets better and better. Let's stay together for always.

A thank you as big as an entire galaxy to Gin, who cheered for me every step of the way. You believed in my words so hard I had to believe it myself. My pep talker, my banisher of doubts, and always my friend.

Thank you to my cover artist and dear friend, Jen Lightfoot! The cover came out perfectly, just like I knew it would when I first asked you to do it. Your work astonishes me with its technical skill, but even more than that, I love the dark dreams you bring to life.

You can contact Jen for commissions and admire her work on her website—
   www.jenlightfoot.com

Thank you to my beta readers, Kia S. and Maz Hedgehog. Thank you for your suggestions and questions. Your clarity and attention to detail was invaluable and I am so grateful to you both for taking the time to help me with this work.

Thank you to the members of my writing group for all your help as I inched towards the finish line.

Thank you to Book Twitter, where everyone really does want you to write a book.

And finally, a thank you to all my Twitter followers. Thank you for being interested in the weird things I think about while I'm waiting for the bus. Y'all made me feel like maybe someone would want to read my brain rumbles if I took the time to pull them together.

I appreciate you.

ABOUT THE AUTHOR

Ali Thompson is the Bill Nye of fat girls. She is the creator of Ok2BeFat, which by an amazing coincidence, is the name of her YouTube channel.

Ali is a fat activist, writer, YouTuber, and collage artist. She is a bisexual queer who lives in Philadelphia with her husband Josh and their many cats.

You can find her on Twitter at @Artists_Ali, where she probably just said something weird.

Find out more at alithompson.net

Printed in Great Britain
by Amazon

44912092R00030